D1226946

the HILLBILLY BIGFOOT
Paranormal Survival Guide

Stories and Art by
Christopher Epling

BY BILL McCURRY

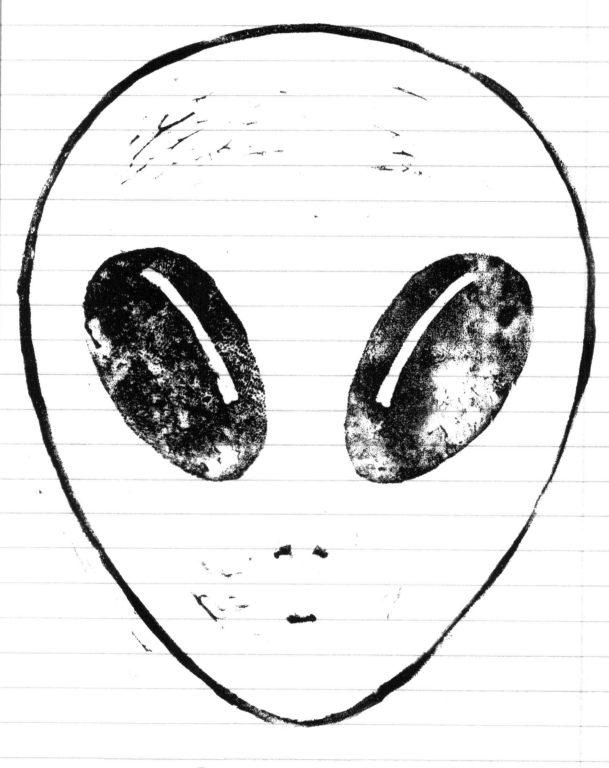

PARANORMAL
SURVIVAL GUIDE

COPYRIGHT © 2020 CHRISTOPHEREPLING.COM
STORIES AND ART BY CHRISTOPHER EPLING.
COVER COLORIST: GABRIEL ELSWICK; ELSWICKVISUALYARNS@HOTMAIL
ALL RIGHTS RESERVED. PLEASE ASK BEFORE USING ANY PORTION OF THIS BOOK.
TO REQUEST PERMISSION, PLEASE EMAIL EPLINGILLUSTRATIONS@GMAIL
EDITOR: RUSS CASSADY
HARDBOUND COPYRIGHT: 978-0-9893574-5-6
LIBRARY OF CONGRESS CONTROL NUMBER: 2020923388
FIRST EDITION: DECEMBER 2020
PRINTED IN THE UNITED STATES BY BOOKMASTERS, ASHLAND OH
PO BOX 183 REGINA, KY 41559
WWW.CHRISTOPHEREPLING.COM

WASHINGTON, DC

HERE IN THIS TOWN, HUSHED CONVERSATIONS ABOUT CLANDESTINE GROUPS AREN'T THAT UNCOMMON AT ALL.

IN THE LATE *1940's*, AN ALLEGED UNITED STATES ARMY AIR FORCE BALLOON CRASHED NEAR A SMALL TOWN IN ROSWELL, NEW MEXICO.

THE CONSPIRACY THEORY ABOUT THE 'MEN IN BLACK'- A SMALL GROUP DEVOTED TO KEEPING SECRETS, SECRET- STARTED THEN AND THERE.

I EXPECT EACH OF YOU ARE FAMILIAR WITH THE REPORT?

YES, SIR. WE'VE READ IT MANY TIMES NOW.

THIS SHOULDN'T BE ANY TROUBLE AT ALL FOR US TO HANDLE.

IS THAT SO? DO YOU REALIZE THAT A SIMPLE COUNTRY BUMPKIN CREATED THIS?

HOMEMADE BOOKS WITH THE NATION'S DEEPEST AND DARKEST SECRETS.

I WANT TO KNOW HOW!

WHOEVER THIS 'BILL' IS, WE WILL FIND HIM. ONCE WE ARE FINISHED WITH HIM, HE WILL BE HAPPY TO GIVE UP HIS PUBLISHING DREAMS.

A PLACE CALLED 'SANDY VALLEY' SOUNDS NICE.

A SMALL TOWN IN APPALACHIA. VERY ISOLATED, REMOTE, AND BUCOLIC SETTING. WE HAVE HAD PAST INTERACTIONS WITH THESE 'TYPES' IN POINT PLEASANT. NOTHING AT ALL WE CAN'T TAKE CARE.

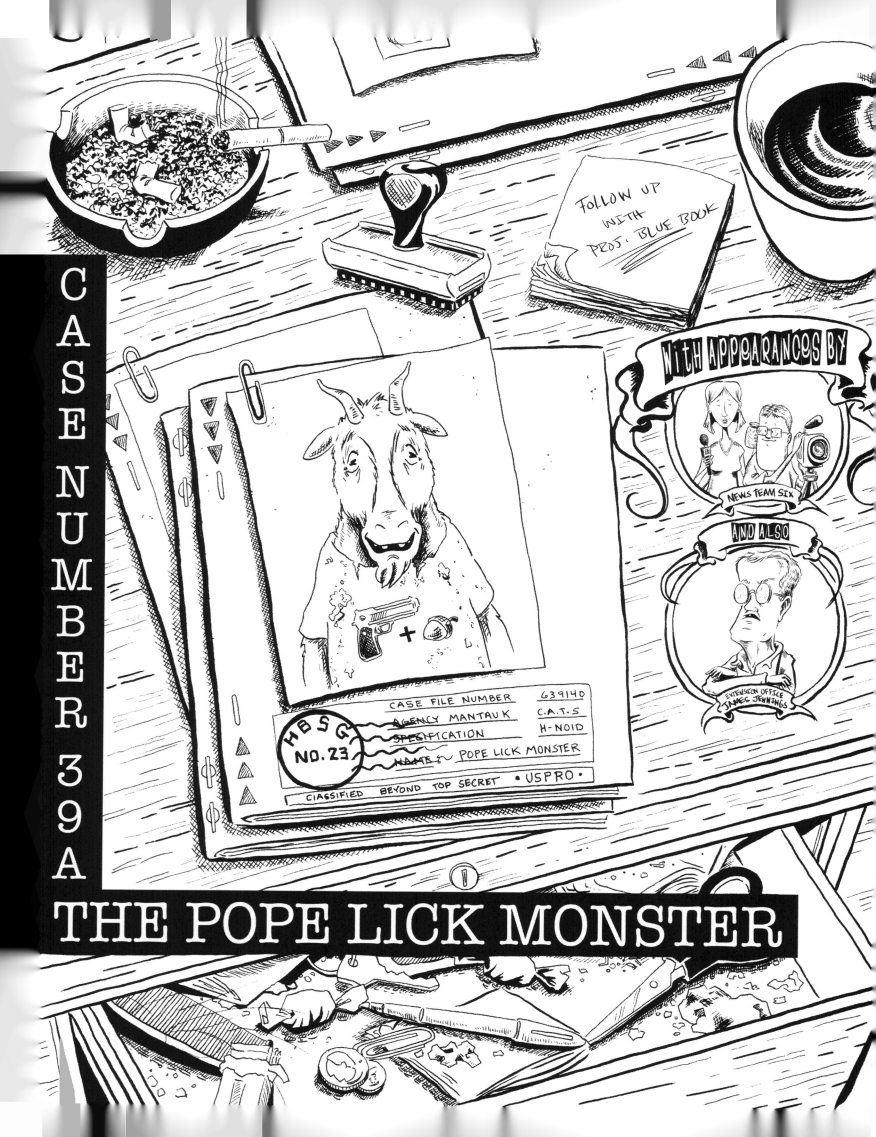

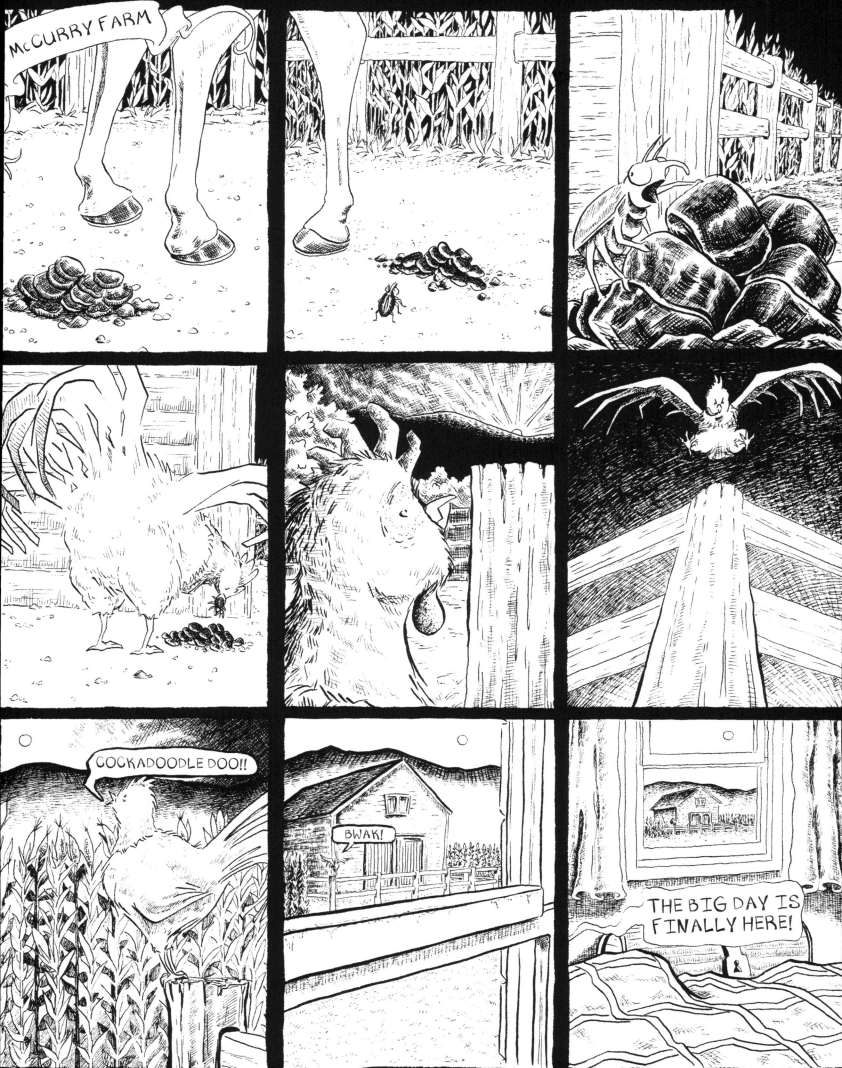

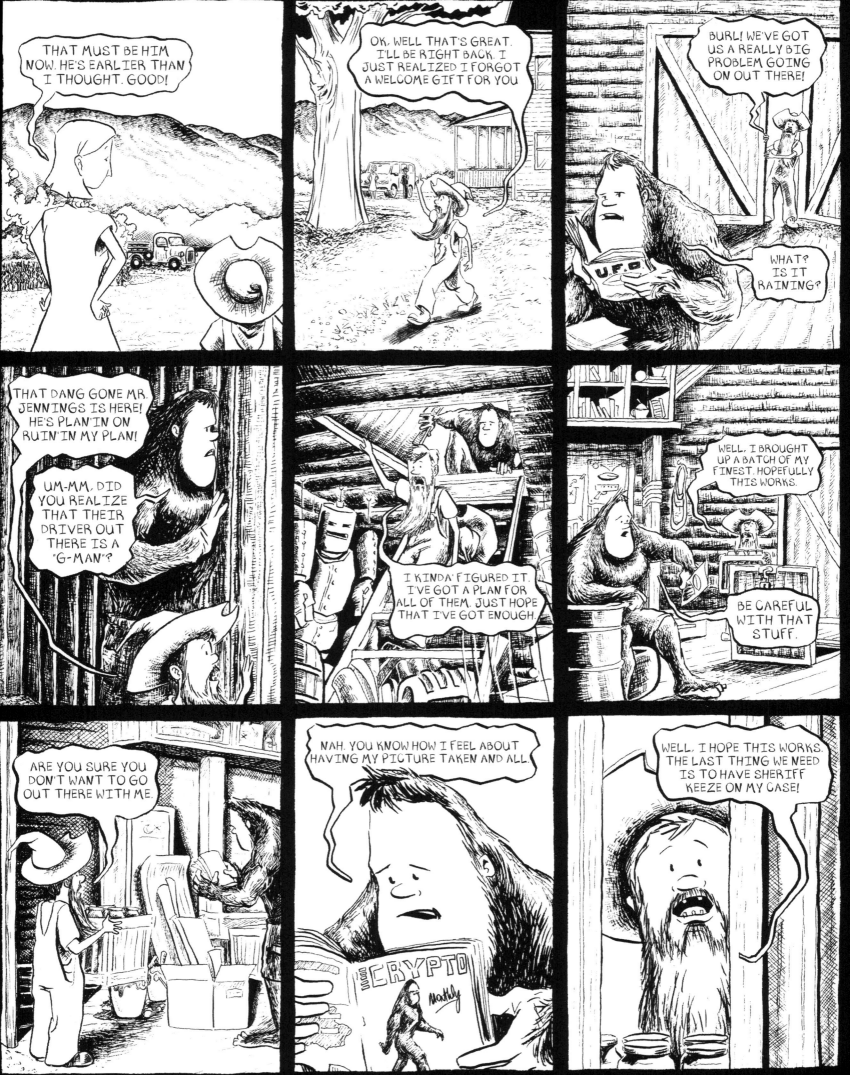

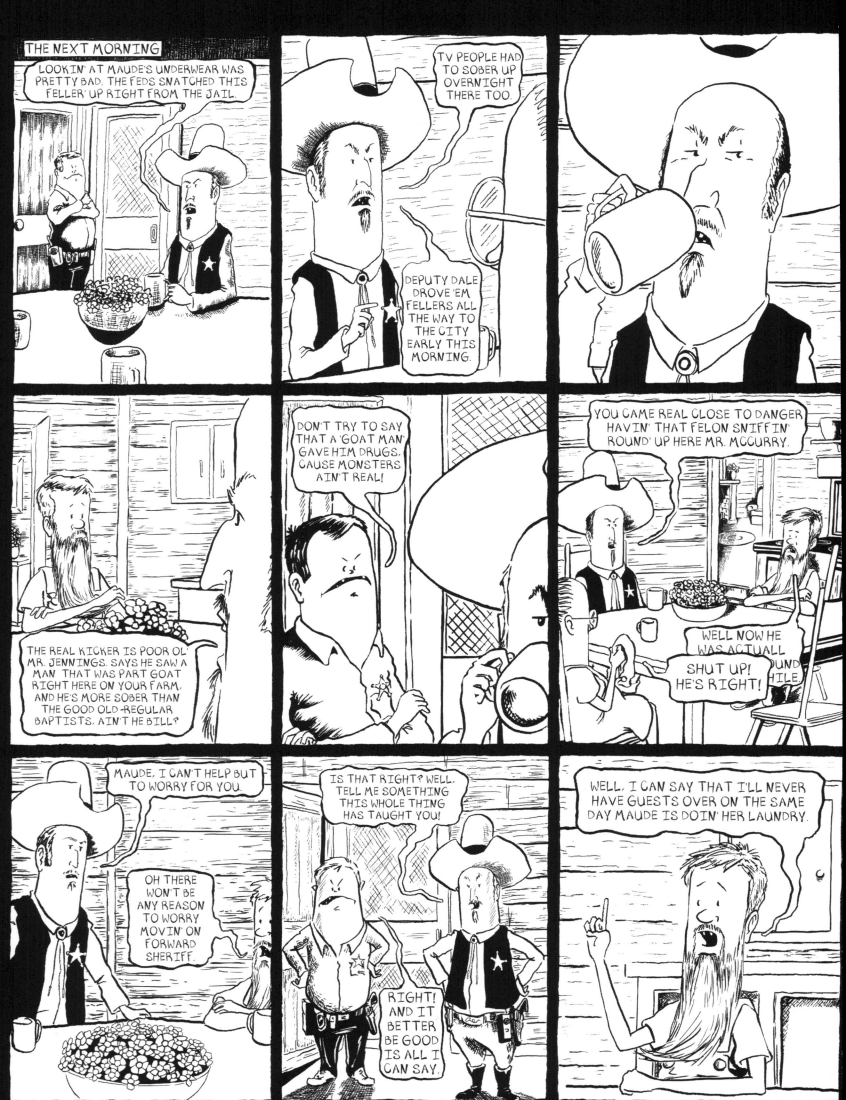

Maude McCoy's Apple Fritters

Ingredients

* Vegetable oil for deep frying
* 2 cups Original Bisquick™ mix
* 1/2 cup cold water
* 1 egg
* 1/4 cup granulated sugar
* 1 teaspoon ground cinnamon
* 1 large unpeeled Granny Smith apple, chopped (about 1 3/4 cup)
* 1/4 cup powdered sugar

First, In deep fryer or four quart heavy saucepan, heat oil to 350°F.

Next, In large bowl, stir Bisquick mix, water, egg, granulated sugar and cinnamon. Fold in apple. Working in batches, drop batter by tablespoonfuls in to hot oil. Cook two to three minutes, turning occasionally, or until golden brown. Use a metal slotted spoon to remove fritters from oil; drain on paper towels.

Last, Before serving, sprinkle fritters with powdered sugar.

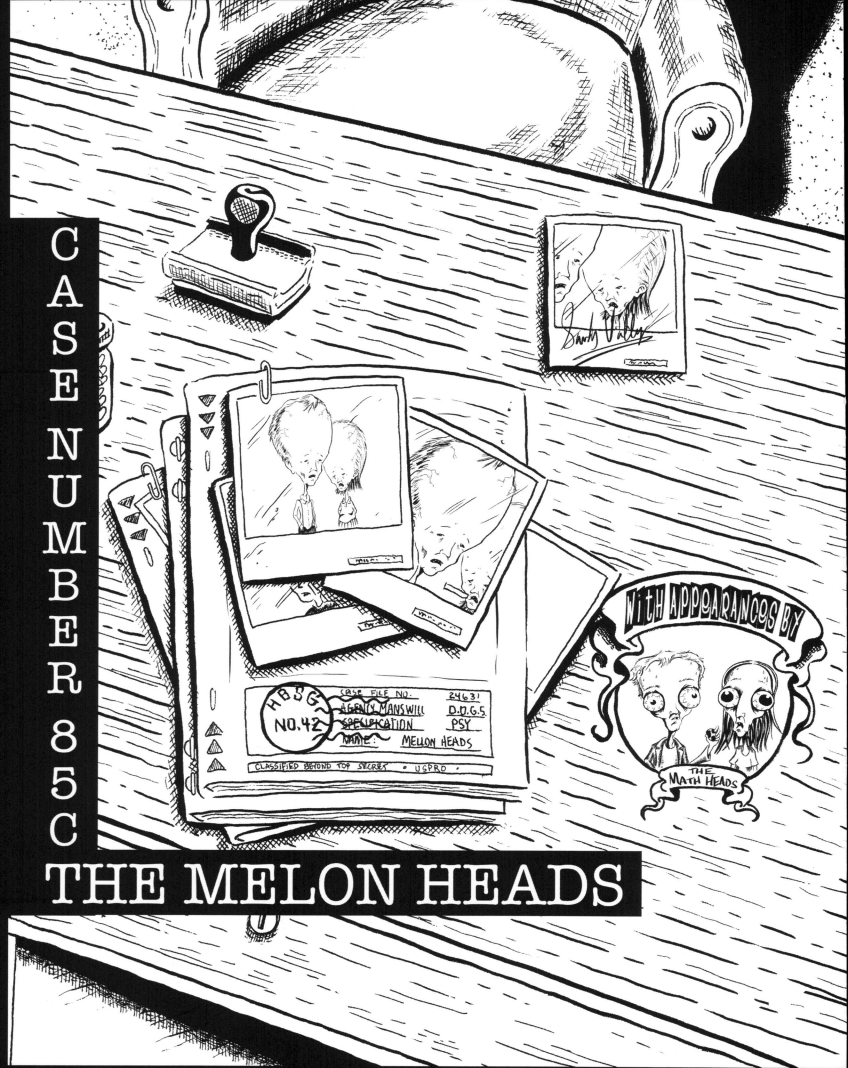

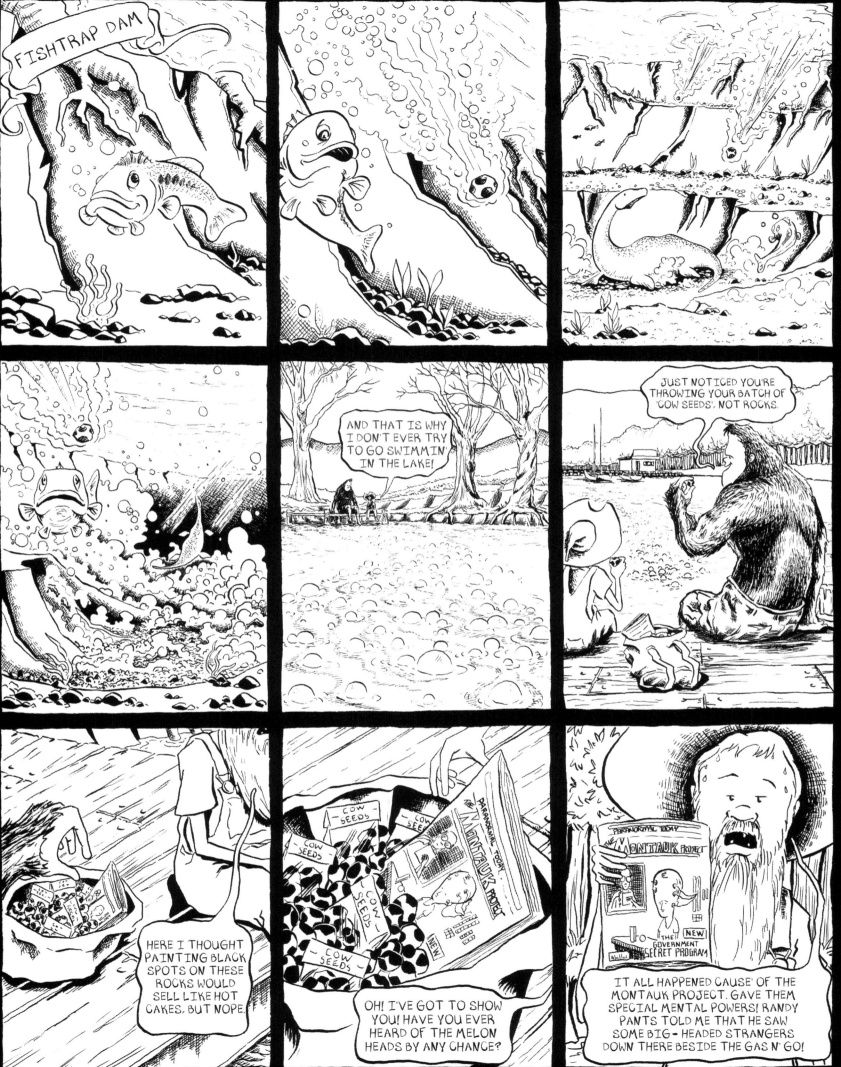

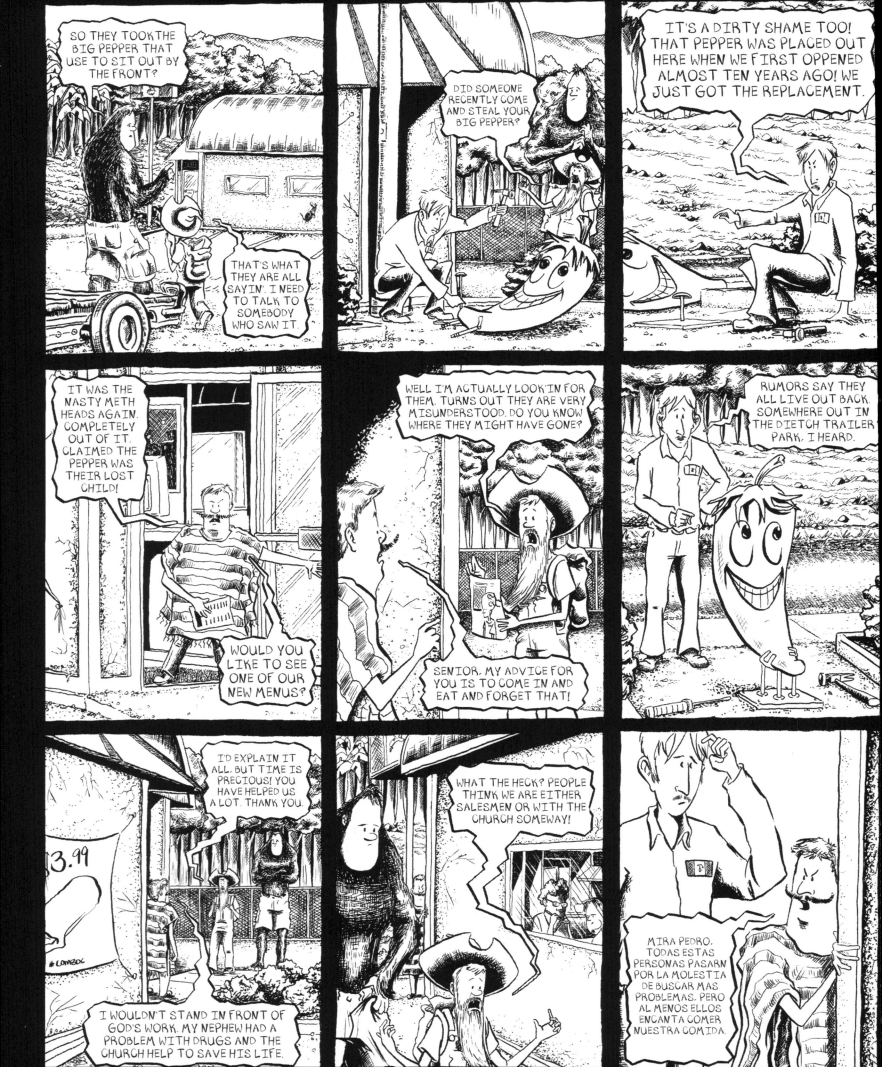

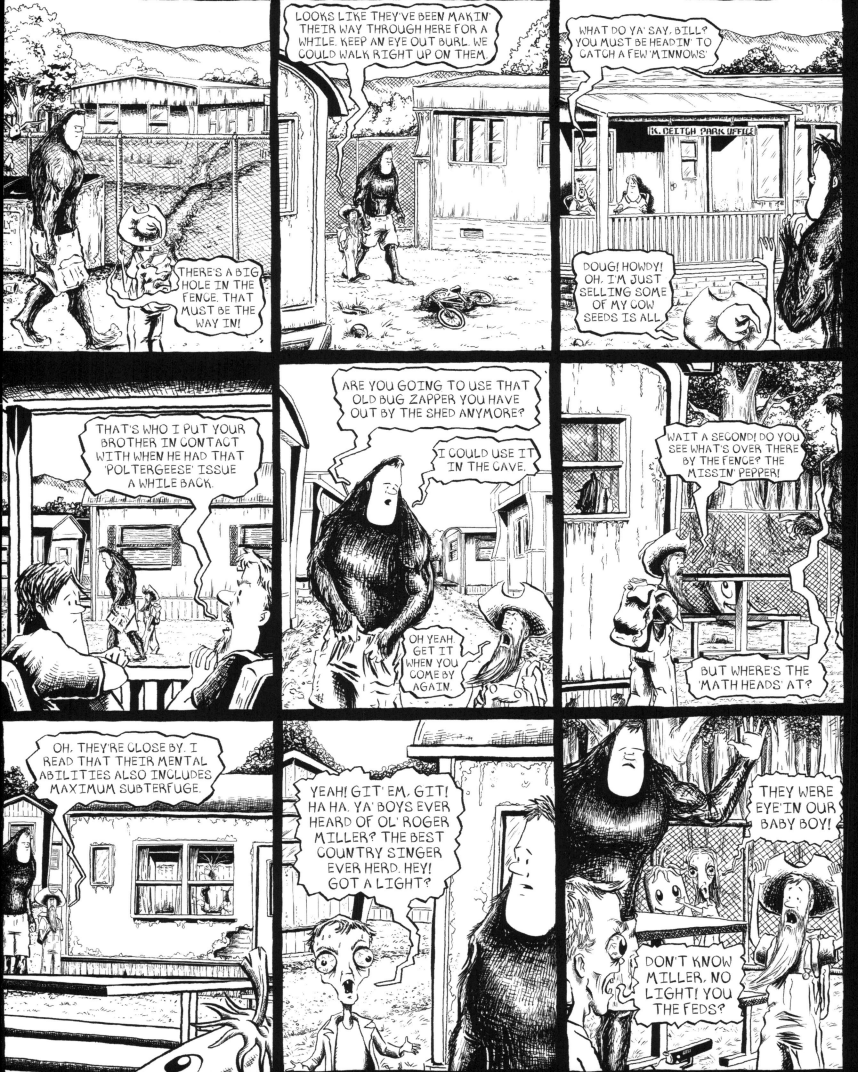

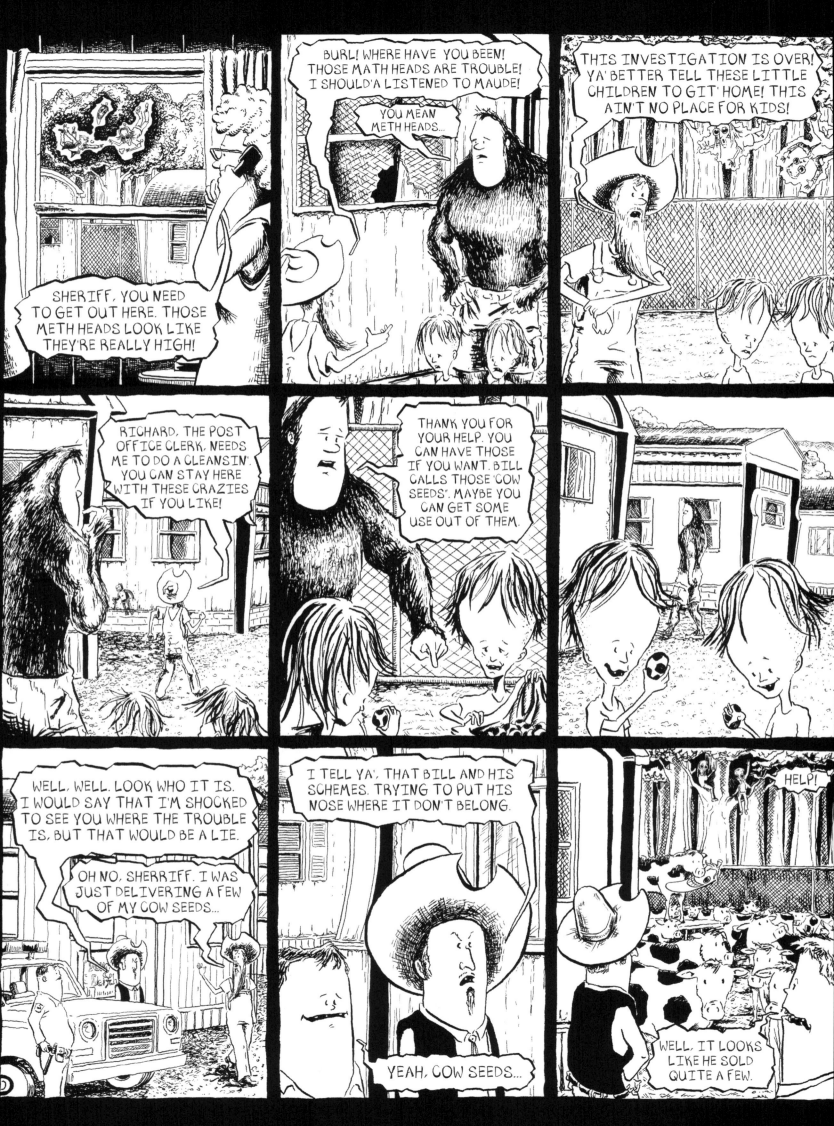

SANDY VALLEY TIMES

EARL RATLIFF

EDITOR

RECENTLY THE SLEEPY HOLLER ON MARROWBONE WAS ROCKED AWAKE WITH AN EXPLOSION THE LIKES OF WHICH SANDY VALLEY HAS NEVER SEEN. THE AUTHORITIES ON THE MATTER CLAIM A METEOR CRASHED DOWN THROUGH THE ATMOSPHERE, STRIKING A SMALL POTATO PATCH BELONGING TO MR. BILL MCCURRY. THE SPACE ROCK WAS FOLLOWED BY A LARGE GREEN FLORESCENT TRAIL WHICH ENDED UP ILLUMINATING THE FALL NIGHT SKY.

AN EXCERPT FROM AN ARTICLE WRITTEN BY EARL RATLIFF

the Potato incident

SINCE THE INCIDENT TOOK PLACE, MR. MCCURRY HAS INSISTED THAT THE IDYLLIC SETTING SURROUNDING HIS OTHERWISE QUAINT FARM HAS BEEN INVADED BY STRANGE HAPPENINGS FRINGING ON THE EDGE OF REALITY ITSELF. FROM ELEVATING MILK COWS, TO RAVENOUS GEESE, MR. MCCURRY'S CLAIMS ARE ALL DOCUMENTED WITHIN THE QUARTERLY SELF PUBLISHED INFORMATIONAL BOOKLET TITLED "THE HILLBILLY PARANORMAL SURVIVAL GUIDE", FROM WHICH HE ALSO OFFERS, FOR A SMALL FEE, SERVICES CENTERING ON SUCH PECULIARITIES.

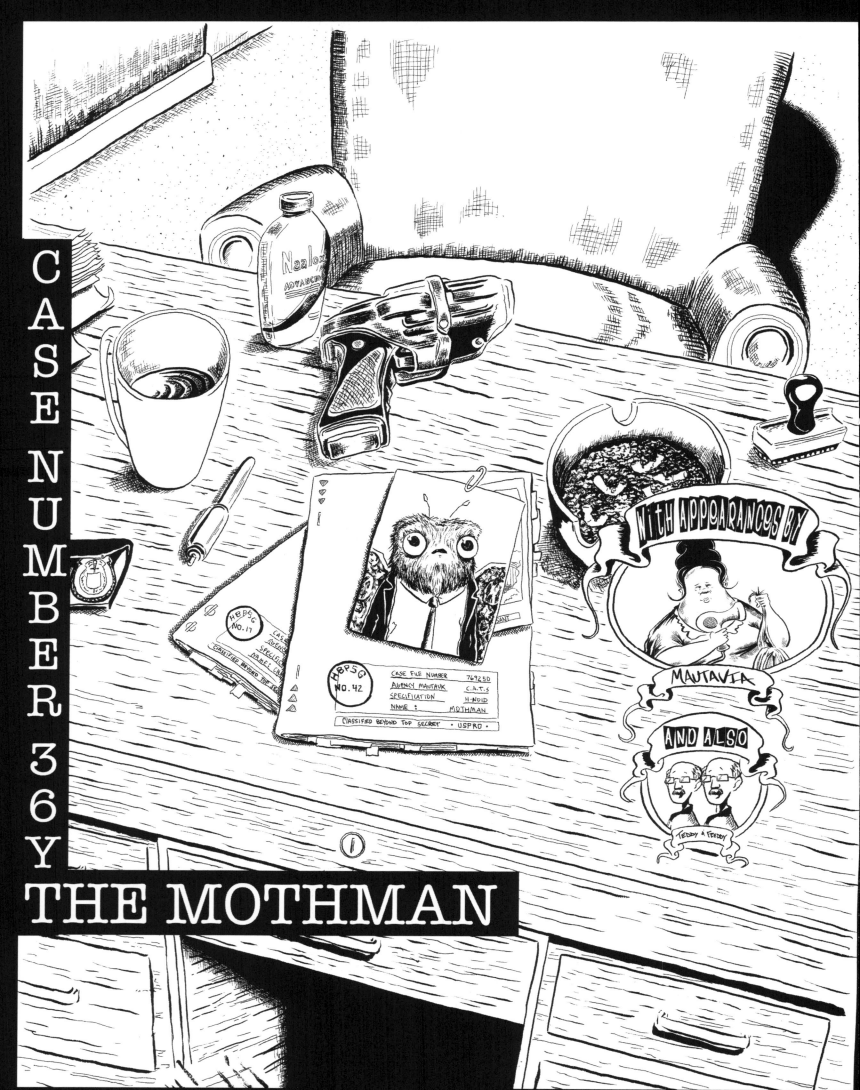

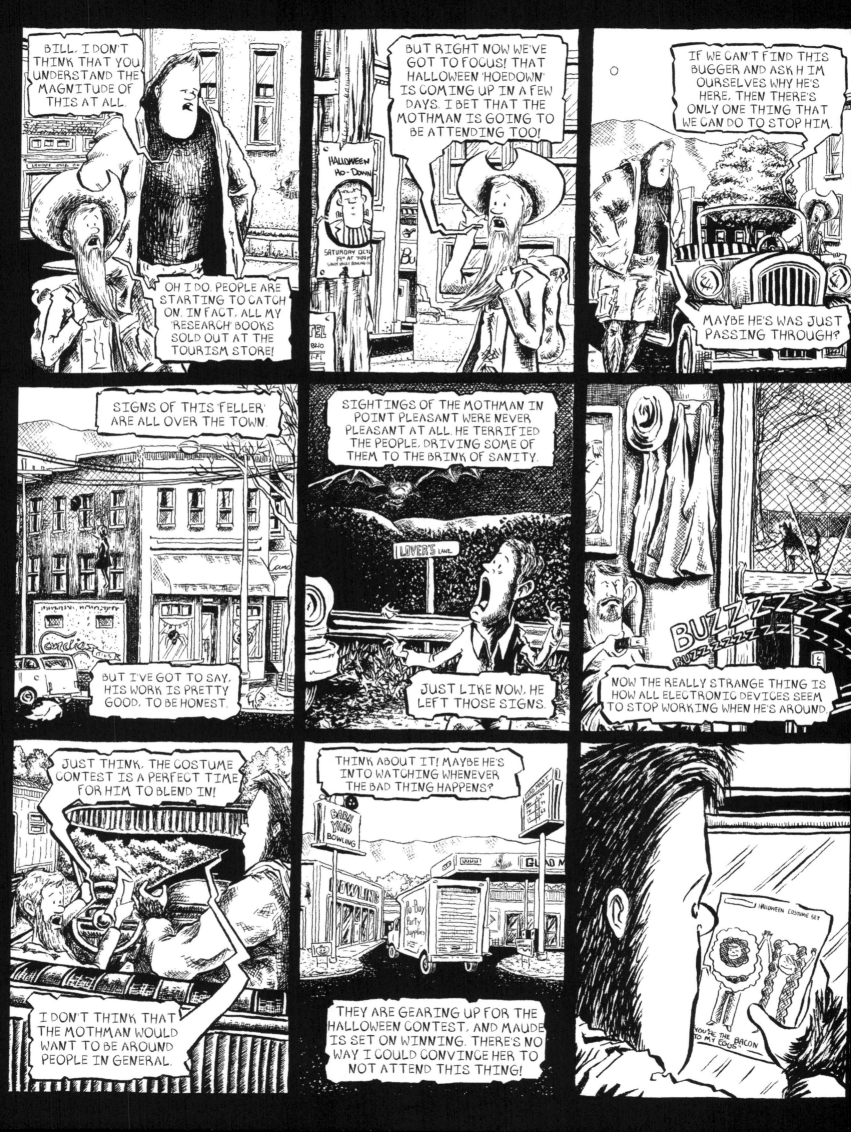

Notes FOR RESEARCH

WED:
CALL MR.
DEITCH. WHERE
IS MY HAT?

HAVE TO
PRACTICE
KNIFE
THROWIN'!?

MAUDE'S GROCERY LIST
- APPLES
- BREAD
- FLOUR
- ANT KILLER
- TIN FOIL

IDEA FOR THROWING BOARD:

PAGE 1

PANEL 1: FIRST TIME I ACTUALLY WENT AND RESEARCHED WHAT COW-POO LOOKS LIKE

PANEL 6: THE FIRST VERSION OF THE H.B.P.S.G. WAS IN THE FORM OF A MINI-COMIC, WHERE BILL IS VISITED BY ALIENS AND MAUDE WAS ABDUCTED. I WANTED TO START THIS BOOK IN THE BEDROOM TOO.

PAGE 2

PANEL 2: MY INTEREST IN THE PARANORMAL STARTED WITH THE NEPHILIM - GENESIS 6:4. MY UNCLE WROTE A GREAT BOOK ABOUT THE SUBJECT. I'VE ALWAYS ADMIRED HIM.

PANEL 8: I STRUGGLED WITH THE "LOOK" OF BURL THE BIGFOOT A LOT. I DIDN'T KNOW IF HE NEEDED CLOTHES OR NOT. AFTER DRAWING HIM A LOT, IT WAS EVIDENT THAT HE DID...

PAGE 5

PANEL 5: A THROW-BACK TO EARLY IRON MAN IN THE FAR RIGHT CORNER OF THE BASEMENT.

PAGE 6

PANEL 7: EVERYONE KNOWS THAT MOONSHINE IS AS CONNECTED TO EASTERN KENTUCKY AS THE HATFIELD AND McCOY FUED. STEREOTYPES ARE TERRIBLE, BUT I LEARNED THAT OFTEN THEY ARE BASED, IN-PART, TO SOME REALITY. SO, YES, FOLKS STILL MAKE THE STUFF YET TODAY.

PAGE 7

PANEL 9: THERE'S NO BETTER SMELL THAN LAUNDRY THAT HAS DRIED OUTDOORS.

PAGE 8

PANEL 6: JAMES JENNINGS IS A THROW-BACK TO MY YOUNGER DAYS WHEN I USE TO PARTICIPATE WITH 4-H A LOT. COUNTY EXTENSION OFFICERS WOULD JUDGE THE ENTRIES FOR THE DIFFERENT COMPETITIONS. I LOVED WINNING RIBBONS FOR MY ARTWORK.

PAGE 9

PANEL 3: "POPE LICK" IS A TRUE LEGEND BASED IN KENTUCKY. I WANTED TO GIVE HIM A LOT OF PERSONALITY, SO THERE'S A DESIGN ON HIS SHIRT THAT TELLS A LOT ABOUT HIM.

PAGE 10

PANEL 1: MY UNCLE TOMMY WAS A DEPUTY SHERIFF IN THE COUNTY I LIVE IN. ALTHOUGH THESE CHARACTERS AREN'T BASED ON HIM, I HAD TO INCLUDE A DEPUTY OUT OF RESPECT. NOT TO MENTION I GREW-UP ON A LITTLE BIT OF THE ANDY GRIFFITH SHOW.

PAGE 13

PANEL 1: OH THE FISHTRAP DAM ... A REAL PLACE THAT HAS DEEP ROOTS TO MY CHILDHOOD.

*TAKE MORE GUIDES TO TOURISM

SCARY AND MEAN

P. GEESE

- LEARNED THAT THE CRUMB METHOD WON'T WORK...

PAGE 14

PANEL 9: THERE IS A SUPER POPULAR MEXICAN JOINT IN MY HOMETOWN. WHEN I HAD TO SELECT A TOPIC RACIST RANDY WOULD BE SO FOCUSED ON, I HAD TO GO WITH EL AZULE GRANDE FOR MY INSPIRATION.

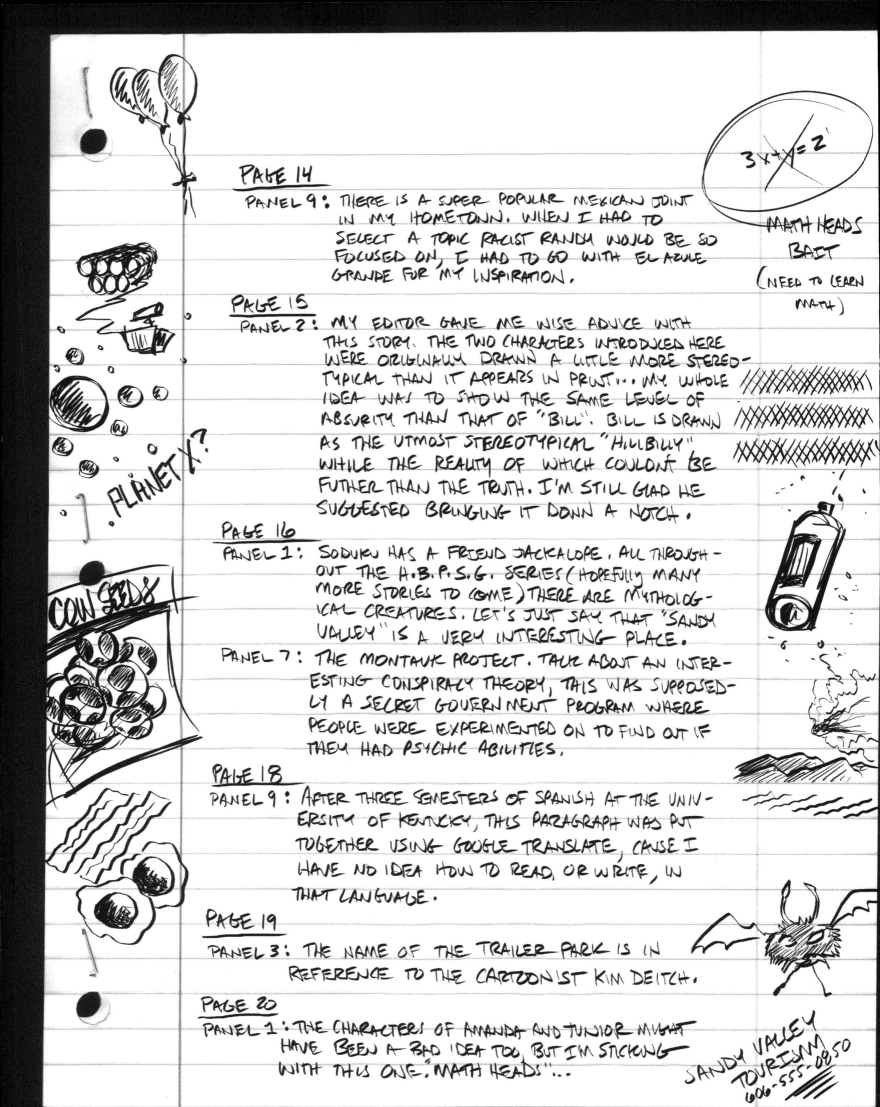

$3x + y = 2$

MATH HEADS BAIT

(NEED TO LEARN MATH)

PAGE 15

PANEL 2: MY EDITOR GAVE ME WISE ADVICE WITH THIS STORY. THE TWO CHARACTERS INTRODUCED HERE WERE ORIGINALLY DRAWN A LITTLE MORE STEREO-TYPICAL THAN IT APPEARS IN PRINT... MY WHOLE IDEA WAS TO SHOW THE SAME LEVEL OF ABSURDITY THAN THAT OF "BILL". BILL IS DRAWN AS THE UTMOST STEREOTYPICAL "HILLBILLY" WHILE THE REALITY OF WHICH COULDN'T BE FUTHER THAN THE TRUTH. I'M STILL GLAD HE SUGGESTED BRINGING IT DOWN A NOTCH.

PAGE 16

PANEL 1: SODUKU HAS A FRIEND JACKALOPE. ALL THROUGH-OUT THE H.B.P.S.G. SERIES (HOPEFULLY MANY MORE STORIES TO COME) THERE ARE MYTHOLOG-ICAL CREATURES. LET'S JUST SAY THAT "SANDY VALLEY" IS A VERY INTERESTING PLACE.

PANEL 7: THE MONTAUK PROJECT. TALK ABOUT AN INTER-ESTING CONSPIRACY THEORY, THIS WAS SUPPOSED-LY A SECRET GOVERNMENT PROGRAM WHERE PEOPLE WERE EXPERIMENTED ON TO FIND OUT IF THEY HAD PSYCHIC ABILITIES.

PAGE 18

PANEL 9: AFTER THREE SEMESTERS OF SPANISH AT THE UNIV-ERSITY OF KENTUCKY, THIS PARAGRAPH WAS PUT TOGETHER USING GOOGLE TRANSLATE, CAUSE I HAVE NO IDEA HOW TO READ, OR WRITE, IN THAT LANGUAGE.

PAGE 19

PANEL 3: THE NAME OF THE TRAILER PARK IS IN REFERENCE TO THE CARTOONIST KIM DEITCH.

PAGE 20

PANEL 1: THE CHARACTERS OF AMANDA AND JUNIOR MIGHT HAVE BEEN A BAD IDEA TOO, BUT I'M STICKING WITH THIS ONE. "MATH HEADS"...

PLANET X?

COW SEEDS

SANDY VALLEY TOURISM 606-555-0850

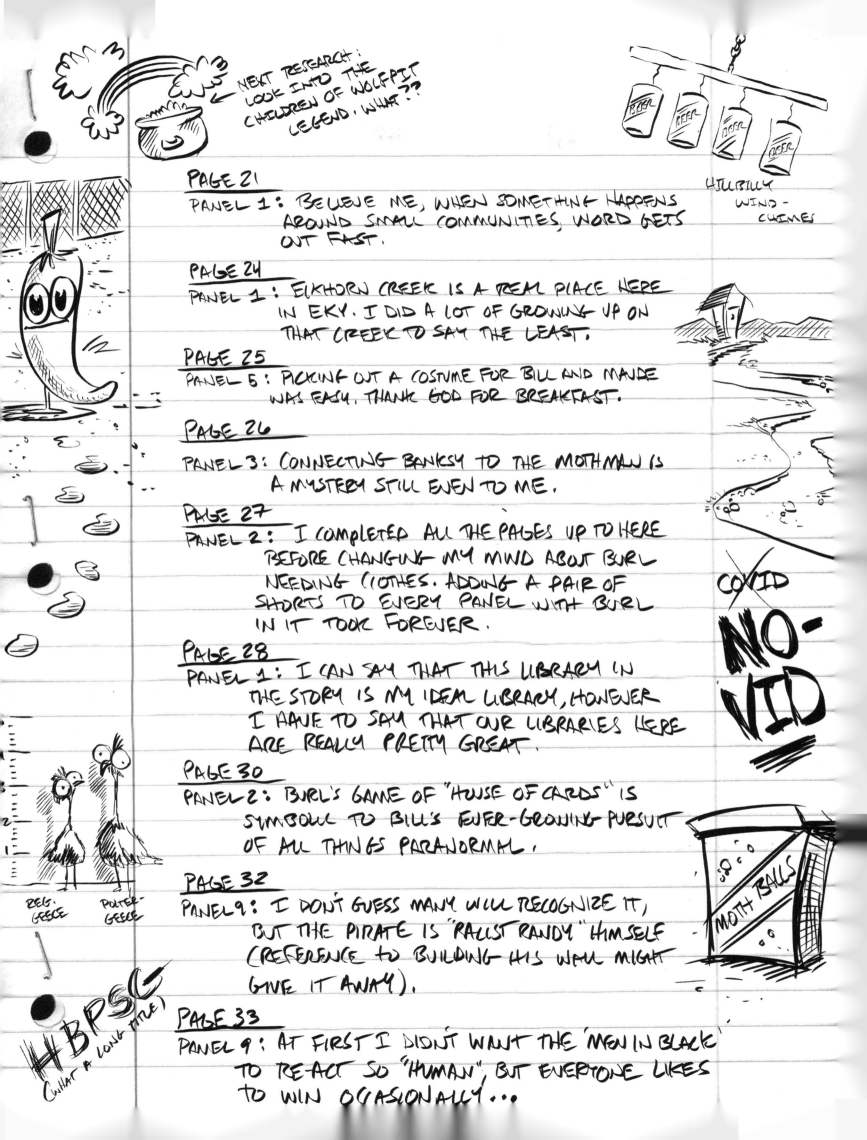

← NEXT RESEARCH:
LOOK INTO THE
CHILDREN OF WOLFPIT
LEGEND, WHAT??

HILLBILLY
WIND-
CHIMES

PAGE 21

PANEL 1: BELIEVE ME, WHEN SOMETHING HAPPENS AROUND SMALL COMMUNITIES, WORD GETS OUT FAST.

PAGE 24

PANEL 1: ELKHORN CREEK IS A REAL PLACE HERE IN EKY. I DID A LOT OF GROWING UP ON THAT CREEK TO SAY THE LEAST.

PAGE 25

PANEL 5: PICKING OUT A COSTUME FOR BILL AND MAUDE WAS EASY. THANK GOD FOR BREAKFAST.

PAGE 26

PANEL 3: CONNECTING BANKSY TO THE MOTHMAN IS A MYSTERY STILL EVEN TO ME.

PAGE 27

PANEL 2: I COMPLETED ALL THE PAGES UP TO HERE BEFORE CHANGING MY MIND ABOUT BURL NEEDING CLOTHES. ADDING A PAIR OF SHORTS TO EVERY PANEL WITH BURL IN IT TOOK FOREVER.

PAGE 28

PANEL 1: I CAN SAY THAT THIS LIBRARY IN THE STORY IS MY IDEAL LIBRARY, HOWEVER I HAVE TO SAY THAT OUR LIBRARIES HERE ARE REALLY PRETTY GREAT.

COVID
NO-VID

PAGE 30

PANEL 2: BURL'S GAME OF "HOUSE OF CARDS" IS SYMBOLIC TO BILL'S EVER-GROWING PURSUIT OF ALL THINGS PARANORMAL.

PAGE 32

PANEL 9: I DON'T GUESS MANY WILL RECOGNIZE IT, BUT THE PIRATE IS "RACIST RANDY" HIMSELF (REFERENCE TO BUILDING HIS WALL MIGHT GIVE IT AWAY).

MOTH BALLS

REG. GEESE   POLTER-GEESE

#BPSC
(WHAT A LONG TITLE)

PAGE 33

PANEL 9: AT FIRST I DIDN'T WANT THE 'MEN IN BLACK' TO REACT SO "HUMAN", BUT EVERYONE LIKES TO WIN OCCASIONALLY...